Published in Great Britain by Brimax,
An imprint of Autumn Publishing Group
Appledram Barns, Chichester, PO20 7EQ

Published in the US by Byeway Books Inc,
Lenexa KS 66219 Tel 866.4BYEWAY
www.byewaybooks.com

Original manuscript by Hilary Lazell
Abridged by Lynne Gibbs
Illustrated by Angela Mills

Printed in China

Hippo Needs Help

Illustrated by Angela Mills

BRIMAX

Harry Hippo, who lives deep in the jungle, is one of the kindest, friendliest animals you could ever meet. But he is also one of the dirtiest, smelliest animals you could ever meet!

Whenever his mother calls, "Time for you to bathe in the lake, little one," Harry runs the other way, as fast as he can!

"Oh, whatever am I going to do with my dirty, muddy, smelly son?" sighed Harry's mother.

"If you don't have a bath soon, no-one will play with you," said Harry's mother as she tucked him up in bed that night.

"Of course they will!" laughed Harry.

Holding her nose, Mrs Hippo kissed Harry goodnight. "Oh, dear," she sighed. "Harry Hippo needs help! He seems to be the only one who doesn't care how awful he smells!"

Early next morning, Harry ran down to a sticky mud hole! Over and over he rolled in the slimy, smelly mud, until he was covered in the smelly stuff!

Then, as a swarm of flies followed close behind him, Harry walked home.

Of course, everyone else, including his friends, stayed well out of Harry's way!

One day, on his way to the mud hole,
Harry saw his friends whispering to
one another.

"Harry Hippo needs help!" whispered
Jenny Giraffe. "He really is very dirty and smelly."

"Shh, here comes Harry now," said Ella Elephant.

"We're sorry we can't stop and play with you
but we're late for the party!" said Timmy Tiger.

"Party? What party?" called Harry, as his
friends ran off through the jungle.

Back home, Harry told his mother what had happened. "My friends have gone to a party without me," he sighed. "No-one wants to be my friend!"

"Oh, of course they do!" said Harry's mother. "Perhaps if you bathe in the lake and make yourself smell nice, they will invite you to the party."

"Bathe?" gasped Harry. "Never! I shall find the party without their help!"

Before his mother could stop him, Harry ran off into the jungle. Soon he came to a clearing.

'WELCOME TO THE PARTY' read a banner, hanging between two trees.

"Wow! Look at that!" laughed Harry when he saw all the pretty balloons and party food.

But just as he was about to take a closer look, Granny Elephant came crashing through the trees.

"Go away! Shoo!" roared Granny Elephant. "You're far too dirty and smelly to come to our party!"

As the elephant chased after him, poor Harry ran back through the jungle, with only a swarm of flies to keep him company.

"Go on! Be off with you!" called Granny Elephant, when Harry stopped for a rest. "I can still smell you from here, you know!"

Finding a quiet spot, Harry cried more than he had ever cried before.

As great big tears ran down his cheeks and made a puddle on the grass, Harry Hippo bowed his head. Everyone is right, he thought to himself, I am a dirty, smelly hippo!

At last, when he had squeezed the very last tear from his eyes, Harry gave himself a shake. It was time for him to go home.

Not noticing where he was going, Harry walked in a big circle – and found himself back at the party!

"Look! It's our friend, Harry!" called Timmy Tiger.

"Wow!" said Jenny Giraffe. "You look very clean and handsome, Harry."

"I do?" said Harry.

"You do!" said his friends.

Harry looked down at his reflection in the lake. It was true – he was clean! His tears had washed the dirt away!

"Oh, I'm so proud of you!" smiled Harry's mother, giving him some ice-cream with a cherry on top.

Now that Harry was clean, even Granny Elephant, who could be rather grumpy, welcomed him to the party!

"This is fun!" laughed Harry as he ate his third bowl of ice-cream.

Harry Hippo promised that he would never go near a mud hole again. Well, not for a few days, anyway!